ROCKETEER

A Novel by Ron Fontes
Based on the Motion Picture from Walt Disney Pictures
Executive Producer Larry Franco
Based Upon the Comic Book Series "The Rocketeer" created by Dave Stevens
Based on the Screenplay by Danny Bilson & Paul De Meo
From a Story by Danny Bilson & Paul De Meo & William Dear
Produced by Lawrence Gordon, Charles Gordon, and Lloyd Levin
Directed by Joe Johnston

NEW YORK

Rocketeer, a junior novelization, is published
by Disney Press, a subsidiary of The Walt Disney Company,
500 South Buena Vista Street, Burbank, California 91521.

Printed and bound in the U.S.A.

Published by Disney Press
114 Fifth Avenue
New York, New York 10011

ISBN 1-56282-065-6
8 7 6 5 4 3 2 1

ROCKETEER

LUCKY LIFTOFF

"Don't let me catch you gettin' fancy first time up," airplane mechanic Peevy Peabody cautioned Cliff Secord.

The cocky young pilot lifted a scornful eyebrow.

"Who, me?" he asked around a mouthful of gum.

The two friends strode across the runway of Chaplin Airfield on a dusty afternoon in 1938. Four men carefully pushed a stubby racing plane from a dark hangar into the California sunshine. They all shared Peevy and Cliff's passion for planes.

In greasy coveralls were Goose, Skeets, Eugene, and Malcolm, an old pilot turned mechanic. Malcolm stopped to mop his red face with a grimy handkerchief. Like Peevy and Cliff, they worked for Bigelow's Air Circus, a racing and stunt-flying show.

Sunlight gleamed on the fresh black-and-yellow paint of the brand-new GeeBee Racer. The little plane was not much more than a gigantic engine with wings and a tiny cockpit. It crouched like an aggressive animal eager to spring into the air.

Peevy and Cliff waved to the crowd of a dozen or so fliers and mechanics gathered to watch the plane's first flight.

"Remember, she stalls at around one hundred," Peevy said. "Keep your air speed up or she'll wallow all over the sky."

"Peevy, I *have* flown a plane or two, you know," Cliff said impatiently.

"This one's a handful. You gotta concentrate on her every second. Sneeze once and you'll be tail up in the beanfield." Peevy waved an excited arm in the direction of the farm beside the airport. Cliff glanced at the dusty field and stuck his chewing gum on the GeeBee's tail rudder.

"That's fresh paint," Peevy remarked.

"You want me to crash?" Cliff asked.

"You and your lame-brained superstitions.

Chewing gum won't keep you up in the air," Peevy scoffed.

Cliff ignored his grouchy friend. He knew Peevy was just nervous. The young man climbed up and squeezed into the tight cockpit of the powerful plane. As he settled in, Goose lowered the canopy over Cliff.

"Treat her right and she'll fly us all the way to the Nationals," Peevy said proudly. It was Cliff and Peevy's dream to win the National Air Races.

Cliff smiled. "Let's make some history."

Cliff's smile spread to Peevy's face. He stepped back and flashed a thumbs-up to Cliff as the canopy was fastened.

"Switch on!" Cliff cried, returning the gesture.

"Crank her up, Skeets!" Peevy yelled.

Skeets spat on his palms, seized the propeller, and yanked hard. The motor caught on the first try and the sweet thunder of 450 horses filled the air.

Peevy plucked the wad of chewing gum from the plane's tail as he stepped clear. The GeeBee turned and taxied toward its starting position.

Inside the cockpit, Cliff admired the photo taped to his control panel. Beneath the beautiful face and satin gown was the inscription: "With love from your Lady Luck, Jenny." A heart with an arrow through it was drawn around his girlfriend's name.

Indicator needles jumped as Cliff opened the throttle. The pilot was pressed back in his seat as the plane picked up speed, skittered over the asphalt, and leaped into the blue.

Peevy and the mechanics craned their necks to follow the black-and-yellow plane rocketing overhead. The GeeBee tipped its wings in a victory salute and zoomed toward the hilly horizon.

Peevy was smiling and calm while jubilant grease monkeys slapped his back. But then he frowned and looked down. He raised his foot and found a sticky wad of chewing gum on the sole of his shoe.

2

TAILSPINS AND TOMMY GUNS

"Hey, Fitch! You tryin' to save ammo?" yelled FBI agent Wooly Wolinski. He was at the wheel of a speeding sedan. Federal agents and the police were in hot pursuit of a tan roadster.

The police car swerved between the other two cars.

"I can't get a clean shot," Fitch complained. "I wish the black-and-white would get out of our way."

Just then a spray of bullets shredded the police car's tires and sent it spinning like a top. Fitch and Wooly ducked as a barrage of bullets shattered their windshield.

"Be careful what you wish for," Wooly cautioned.

Fitch returned fire.

In the roadster, the wheelman, Wilmer, ducked as his rearview mirror cracked. An odd-shaped stolen suitcase made of leather and brass bounced on the seat beside him.

The triggerman, Lenny, crouched in the back seat of the car, cradling a chattering tommy gun. He stitched a seam of bullets across the sedan's grille. Steam billowed from the G-men's ruptured radiator. Their auto slowed.

Wilmer floored the gas to get to the top of a hill. But a slow farm truck was chugging up the other side! Wilmer whipped the wheel. His car careened off the road in a cloud of dust. Wooly and Fitch bounced behind him in pursuit across the beanfield.

As Lenny reloaded his tommy gun, he spotted a black-and-yellow plane buzzing low. In his panic he was sure the GeeBee held more federal agents. He fired for all he was worth.

Cliff was stunned when bullets ripped the underside of his plane. A bullet cracked the clear canopy. The engine sputtered, and smoke streamed into the cockpit. Cliff tried to stay cool, fighting to keep the GeeBee in the air.

"Don't die on me now!" he begged. "No more surprises."

And just as he spoke, a part popped from the engine. A thick stream of motor oil coated the canopy. He was flying blind! Cliff punched through the cracked glass, and the canopy collapsed. He saw another plane coming right at him!

Cliff yelled and jerked back on the stick. His wheels grazed a billboard advertising the war movie *Wings of Honor*. The tin propeller attached to the billboard's plane spun wildly in his wake.

Down below, the speeding gangsters regained the road and spotted a sign: CHAPLIN AIRFIELD—1 MILE.

"Head for that airstrip! I can fly a plane," Lenny cried.

But the G-men were still right behind them. As Lenny blasted away with his tommy gun, Wilmer veered through an orchard. He steered the slim roadster between two trees.

"It's not gonna make it!" Fitch warned when he saw Wooly was determined to follow the little car. No sooner had he spoken than their sedan was wedged between the trunks.

"Like I said," Fitch declared. Wooly glared at

him and threw the car into reverse. Metal crunched and fenders ripped free.

The roadster screeched to a halt behind an airfield hangar. Wilmer hopped out, clutching the strange suitcase.

"Let's go, Lenny! We can't get caught with—"

But Lenny had been shot. He wasn't going anywhere but to the morgue.

"Lousy Feds," Wilmer muttered. He could hear the straining engine of the agents' sedan barreling across the field.

Frightened and alone, Wilmer rushed into the hangar. His darting, desperate eyes searched for something that looked like what was in his suitcase. Faint hope flickered in his mind when he found the slick cylinder of a vacuum cleaner. He'd make a switch and come back later for his stolen property.

"Something ain't right!" Peevy said, jumping to his feet. His mechanic's ear heard the labored sputter of the GeeBee struggling to stay aloft. The plane wobbled toward the runway, a plume of smoke billowing from its bullet-scarred engine.

Up in the cockpit, Cliff wiped his greasy goggles and peered through the black cloud. He could barely make out the airfield.

Wilmer's roadster raced across the runway. He heard shots and looked behind him. There was the FBI. Fitch was firing away. A bullet struck Wilmer in his shoulder. He turned to find the GeeBee swooping straight at him.

Cliff saw the tan roadster and yanked back on the stick. Wilmer leaped from the doomed auto, leaving the suitcase behind. The roadster's windshield tore the wheels from the bottom of the plane. The GeeBee skidded on its belly in a shower of sparks and shaved metal. The empty roadster careened into a parked fuel truck on the runway's edge. Truck and car exploded in a churning ball of flame and smoke.

Peevy, Goose, and Skeets hurried to the downed plane, carrying fire extinguishers. Malcolm followed close behind. Sirens screamed as a water truck and fire engine roared down the runway toward the exploded fuel truck.

Peevy was first to reach the smashed, smoldering GeeBee.

"Goose! Gimme a hand," the mechanic ordered. He and Goose frantically pried open the jammed cockpit. Skeets and Malcom sprayed the engine before the flames reached the fuel tank.

Cliff snatched Jenny's photo from the cockpit as strong hands pulled him free of the blazing plane. Cliff and Peevy watched their dream of the Nationals go up in smoke—literally.

Within minutes the airfield was crawling with cops and Feds. Cliff and Peevy took off after Wooly and Fitch.

"Let me get this straight," Peevy said to the agents. "You chase some two-bit thugs onto our runway, they crash into my pilot, and it's *our* fault?!"

Wooly scowled at Peevy. "No offense, Pops, but we've got more to worry about than whose fault it was."

"That plane took us three years to build and every dime we had," Peevy said.

Fitch shrugged. "File a complaint with Uncle Sam."

Cliff jumped into the argument. "We can't wait

six months or a year. We make our living with that plane!"

Fitch studied Cliff's furious, smoke-stained face. "So maybe it's time to get a real job."

That was too much for Cliff. He aimed a punch for Fitch's jaw, but Peevy caught his arm. Wooly pushed his angry partner back. They didn't need a riot. Peevy led Cliff away.

"You want to let him get away with assaulting an agent?" Fitch demanded.

"Maybe you had it coming," Wooly said. "Let's get back to work while we still have jobs."

Fitch frowned, but he followed Wooly to the ambulance, where Wilmer moaned on a stretcher. He was bandaged from head to toe. Fitch leaned over him. "Your pal is playing his harp," he said. "If you make it to County General your next stop is Alcatraz. So spill it! Where's the suitcase?"

Wilmer chuckled softly. "Blown to bits."

"Hey, Fitch!" a G-man yelled. "Take a look at this."

A fireman used tongs to extract a twisted, smoking object from the blackened wreck of the roadster.

Fitch and Wooly grimly studied the charred lump of metal. It *looked* like what they were after.

"That's the gizmo, all right," Wooly decided.

Fitch dug a nickel out of his pocket. "Call him, Wooly."

"Why me?" Wooly asked.

"He likes you," Fitch explained.

Wooly sighed and went to find a phone.

SECRETS AND SCHEMES

The famous airplane designer and multimillionaire Howard Hughes was sitting behind his desk in his office, speaking on the phone.

"There's no mistake, Wooly?" he asked. "It was sloppy, but it could have been worse. Right."

He hung up and turned in his chair to face two government officials.

"That was Wolinski," Hughes said. "The agents chased the thieves to an airstrip in the Valley. There was a wreck on the runway. The X-3 was destroyed."

"Better lost than in the wrong hands," said one of the officials. "How soon can you rebuild it?"

"Rebuild it? Not a chance," Hughes said.

"My people in Washington will have something

to say about that," the other official argued, trying to intimidate Hughes.

"Your people want to turn anything that flies into a weapon. It looks like someone else had the same idea." Hughes rifled through a thick portfolio of diagrams. A look of regret passed over his face.

"Sir, I'm afraid we must insist . . ."

"I don't work for the government. I cooperate at my discretion. Two of my best pilots died testing the X-3. How many more would die if you had your way? I'm sorry I ever dreamed it up." The tycoon tossed the plans into the fireplace.

"What will we tell the President?" one of the officials asked.

In the hearth, smoke wafted from the plans and from a watercolor illustration of a flying man soaring above the clouds. Hughes watched sadly as the paper curled and turned to ash.

"Tell him the dream is over. Tell him Howard Hughes said so," the designer declared. As he spoke, the painted sky blackened and the flying man burst into flames.

* * *

"Three hundred gallons!" Peevy screeched. "We don't burn that much fuel in two years." The mechanic stared dumbfounded at the bill that air show boss Otis Bigelow had given him.

"You burned it in two seconds when the fuel truck exploded," Bigelow said. Peevy's mouth wouldn't close, but he couldn't say anything either. The GeeBee destroyed, and this too! He was *not* having a good day.

Cliff jumped in. "I didn't blow up your truck. The guy in the car did."

"Yeah, after bouncing off you," Bigelow said. "Pilots are responsible for a safe landing. You know that."

"Where are we gonna get this kind of dough?" Peevy asked. "The GeeBee's scrapped," he added sadly.

"Look, fellas, I hate to kick you when you're down," Bigelow said in a soothing voice. Peevy perked up. Maybe Bigelow was going to be reasonable.

"But business is business," Bigelow went on. "I'm out of pocket here. Of course, I could always use the old clown act."

Peevy frowned. Cliff scowled, but he was thinking.

"We don't do that anymore," Peevy said flatly.

"Sure we do," Cliff said, ignoring Peevy's glare. It was the only way out. "Fifteen bucks a show, right?"

"Ten," Bigelow said. "Five goes against your fuel bill."

Cliff and Peevy exchanged a glance. They had no choice.

"See it my way or see me in court," Bigelow concluded. "Your clown suit's in the storeroom. First show's at nine. Don't be late." Bigelow left the hangar, puffing a cigar.

"Lousy nickel-nurser," Cliff muttered darkly.

Peevy sputtered like an old engine. "Cliff, are you off your nut? Doin' the clown act means goin' up in 'Mabel.' She's a flying coffin. You said so yourself."

"I'll go easy on her," Cliff promised. "She never let us down before." He pulled out his photo of Jenny and with a grin stuck it on the old biplane's instrument panel.

"The number-five piston's shot!" Peevy fussed.

"She's more spit and baling wire than airplane."

"I can fly a shoebox if it's got wings," Cliff said. He hopped into Mabel. "Ouch!" he yelled, jumping back up. He rummaged under the seat and tugged out a gray duffel bag.

"That's my duffel bag," Peevy said, surprised.

"It's heavy!" Cliff said. He carried the bag to a work table and dropped it with a thump. Cliff opened the bag and he and Peevy stared down at a sleek device that looked like large twin bullets of steel and chrome with leather straps.

Cliff was puzzled. "What do you suppose it is?"

He uncoiled a cable about the length of his arm. On the end was a weird metal T like a flat bracelet with a red button in the center. Curious, Cliff pushed the button.

A blast of flame shot the gizmo off the table. Peevy was knocked to the floor. The cylinders smashed against a rafter, bounced off the ceiling, and zoomed to the floor. With a shower of sparks, the rocket ricocheted off a steel tool cabinet and straight through the wall of Bigelow's office.

Terrified, Cliff and Peevy peered through the

hole. The sputtering rocket speared the back of Bigelow's chair. The powerful engine vibrated and spat fire.

Dodging the intense heat of the flame, Cliff and Peevy ducked into the room. Using a mop handle, Cliff punched the red button. The rocket shut off. Peevy and Cliff sighed with relief. Cliff reached to pull the device from the chair.

"Careful. It's hot!" Peevy cautioned.

Cliff yanked back his fingers, then gingerly touched the sleek shell. "It's still cool!" he marveled.

Cautiously they pried the rocket pack from the easy chair. They carefully carried it back to the workbench.

"Never seen anything like this!" Peevy sniffed the engine. "It burns alcohol. What's it for?"

Cliff's eyes gleamed. He had a hunch. It might be crazy, but he couldn't ignore it. He strapped the rocket pack on his back. They could both see exactly what it was for.

"What went wrong?" Neville Sinclair asked. He was practicing his fencing in the library of his elegant Hollywood Hills mansion. The sharp foil sliced the air as Sinclair glared at gangsters Eddie Valentine, Rusty, and Spanish Johnny.

Valentine's dark eyes glittered. Despite his expensive suit, he still looked like a street tough. He didn't like this English sissy talking to him like this—even if he was a famous movie star.

"The FBI's what went wrong," Eddie said. "They showed up like flies at a picnic. Now Lenny's dead and Wilmer's in County General wrapped up like a mummy. You didn't level with me, mister. This was supposed to be a simple snatch-and-grab."

Sinclair set down his sword. "I'm truly sorry about your boys. But I didn't say it would be simple. And they're supposed to be good at snatch-and-grab."

"They are when they know what they're grabbing," Eddie snapped. "Why are the Feds so interested in this package, anyway?"

"Relax, Eddie," Sinclair cooed.

Eddie exploded. "Relax? I'm not your delivery boy. I wanna know why the merchandise I'm moving is so hot."

"You needn't worry about that," Sinclair said.

"Let's go, boys," Eddie said. The gangsters turned and started for the door.

"It's a rocket," Sinclair stated quietly.

Eddie turned and fixed a skeptical eye on the actor. "A rocket? Like in the funny books?"

"Yes." Sinclair was amused. "Like in the comic books. Now, what happened to it?"

Eddie wasn't sure if he believed Sinclair. "The only one who knows is Wilmer. But the hospital is so thick with cops we can't get near him till the heat dies down."

"I can't wait," Sinclair said. "If you can't get to Wilmer, I'll have to handle it myself."

Eddie's raucous laugh mocked the Englishman. "Mr. Movie Star is gonna waltz past the cops with a fistful of flowers!"

"Not precisely what I had in mind." Sinclair studied the tip of the fencing foil, checking the trueness of the blade.

"You don't need me. I got half a mind to pull out of this deal. My boys are getting hurt and you're not playing straight with me. Pay what you owe me—" Eddie's voice choked off when Sinclair whipped the point of the sword against his neck.

Rusty and Spanish Johnny reached for their guns, but Eddie's raised hand stopped them.

"You'll honor our contract or I'll be very disappointed," Sinclair said dryly. The gangster and the actor locked eyes.

A menacing smile hovered on Eddie's lips. "Try it."

Sinclair burst into laughter. With a quick flick of the foil, he flipped the flower off Eddie's lapel. It landed in Rusty's hands.

"I need the rocket, Eddie. And I need your loyalty."

"Loyalty's extra," Eddie growled.

"Bring me the rocket and your price is doubled. Fair?"

Eddie considered the offer. This was good business. "You know, Sinclair? Someday you could end up kissing fish under the Santa Monica pier."

With that, Eddie and his boys started down the hall. Sinclair watched them go with barely concealed contempt.

"That's a good line, Eddie," Sinclair said mockingly. "May I use it if I ever play a cheap crook?" He threw down the foil.

"Bloody amateurs," he muttered, and opened a secret door. Seated by a radio and decoding machine, Sinclair consulted a codebook. He spoke into a microphone, "I regret to inform you that the package has been delayed. Over."

The decoding machine clacked and chattered. Paper tape unspooled from a slot. A dismayed Sinclair read the message: "RENDEZVOUS CANNOT BE CHANGED." This was impossible!

"I need more time," he begged into the microphone.

Again the answer slithered from the slot: "UNACCEPTABLE. AWAIT FURTHER TRANSMISSION. END."

Sinclair slapped the codebook shut. The bent cross of a Nazi swastika blazed on the cover. Neville Sinclair was a Nazi spy!

He picked up the telephone and dialed. "Yes?" a deep voice answered. "That job we discussed. I'd like you to visit a 'friend' in County General Hospital," Sinclair said. "Room 502."

4

WINGS AND WISHES

A life-size wooden statue of air hero Charles Lindbergh stood on the front lawn of the Lucky Lindy Flight School. That is, until Cliff and Peevy sawed the statue off its base and strapped the rocket pack onto its back. Soon the statue was flying at the end of a chain staked in the middle of the beanfield. Cliff and Peevy grinned with glee.

"If I weren't seeing it I wouldn't believe it," Peevy said.

Cliff saw the stake shaking free of the earth. He leaped to grab the chain, but Peevy pulled him down. "That chain will cut you in half!" he warned.

The shuddering stake was uprooted and the rocket's flame became a bright dot quickly lost among the stars. Cliff and Peevy gazed upward.

"What the . . ." Peevy breathed. He heard a metallic moaning from the sky. The chain snaked down and slammed into the dust.

Cliff mourned. "We should've anchored it to your truck."

Peevy slapped him with his hat. "My truck would be halfway to Cincinnati, you chowderhead!"

The statue returned like a whistling bomb. It missed them by inches and plowed a furrow in the field. The two men raced over and shut the rocket down.

"You'd pay to see a man fly, wouldn't you?" Cliff asked.

Peevy grabbed the statue's feet and tugged it free of the furrow. "I know what you're thinking. Forget it."

They carried the statue to the truck.

"But I'm talking about some real money," Cliff persisted. "Not ten bucks a show! Enough to get us back in the Nationals!"

"Are your eyes painted on? This thing is like strapping nitro to your back. And the Feds are mixed up in this."

"Thanks to them we're flying in the clown act

and scraping nickels," Cliff said. "They owe us."

"Maybe they don't see it that way," Peevy said.

"We'll just borrow the pack till we can buy a new plane. Then we'll give it back, I swear!" Cliff said hastily.

Peevy shook his head, far from convinced. He pointed to the statue's smashed head. "You want to turn your head into a plow? The pack doesn't work!"

"A genius like you can fix it."

Peevy moaned. "We'll need a genius of a lawyer."

"I think we need a helmet," Cliff said.

"I think I got the part!" Jenny said excitedly when Cliff picked her up at Mrs. Pye's Boarding House for Young Actresses.

"That's great," Cliff said. "Do you have lines this time?"

"Just one. But it's to Neville Sinclair," Jenny replied with a sigh. "Now you tell me. How did the GeeBee's first flight go?"

"She flew great," Cliff said. "Landing had a few . . . bumps." Reluctant to break the bad news about his plane, he looked at his watch. "Hey, we've got to hurry if we're going to catch a movie."

"There's a new Neville Sinclair picture," Jenny suggested.

Cliff dismissed the idea. "Aw, he's a sissy."

"Would a sissy get shot down behind enemy lines?" Jenny asked. "The movie is *Wings of Honor.*"

"This I've got to see," Cliff agreed. After all, he had already seen the billboard!

"Whozat? Whozere?" Wilmer whispered fearfully in his darkened hospital room.

A match flamed near his bandaged face. Spooky organ music drifted in from a cop's radio in the hall. Wilmer blinked and wondered if he was having a nightmare.

Curtains billowed in the breeze, fluttering like ghosts. A huge shadow loomed on the wall. The face over Wilmer's bed could have belonged to Frankenstein's monster. Then Wilmer's mind cleared and he recognized the man in his room.

"Lothar! Tell your boss I only answer to Eddie."

Lothar's huge hands scooped Wilmer from the

bed. The gangster gasped in pain. "Okay, ease off. I pulled a switch, see? I hid the package in some old plane at the airfield. Hangar Three." And those were the last words Wilmer ever spoke.

"Oh good, it hasn't started yet," Jenny whispered in the crowded movie theater. Cliff balanced two sodas and popcorn. A newsreel flickered on the screen.

"I wouldn't want to miss a second of Neville Sinclair," Cliff teased as they found two empty seats.

"As rumors of war haunt Europe, Herr Hitler claims to be working for world peace," the newsreel announcer said.

"But he means a piece of the world," Cliff scoffed. People shushed him. On the screen a zeppelin descended from the clouds. The crooked cross of a Nazi swastika decorated its tailfins.

"Here comes the Führer's latest goodwill gesture, the mighty airship *Luxembourg*, on a coast-to-coast goodwill tour of the United States."

"Their last goodwill tour buried half of Europe," Cliff said. Embarrassed, Jenny nudged him.

"First stop, New Jersey," the announcer continued, and the screen showed German airmen handing candy bars to eager children. The captain waved to the camera, grinning broadly. "Welcome, boys," said the announcer. "Look us up when you get to Hollywood!"

After the movie Cliff and Jenny went to the Bulldog Café, near the airfield, and shared their usual booth. Skeets, Goose, and Malcolm warmed the worn leather stools at the counter. The café was actually shaped like a giant bulldog, with a pipe in its mouth and a door in its belly.

"Then—get this, fellas—at the end of the movie he flies over enemy trenches to drop a bottle of champagne," Cliff recounted.

"Let me guess," said Goose. "It hits the general and we win the war. Right?" The regulars guffawed.

"It was symbolic. He was being chivalrous," Jenny said. "It was so romantic, Millie. I cried and cried," Jenny told the owner, who was cooking at the grill. "Neville was wonderful!"

"Neville!" Cliff said. "The guy's never been up in a plane, much less flown one."

"Who cares?" Millie asked. "He's a living doll!"

Flying ace Cliff Secord with his GeeBee Racer.

Gangster Luther fires at the FBI while Wilmer drives. They've stolen a rocket pack from none other than millionaire/inventor Howard Hughes!

The gangsters' car hits the air show's fuel tank.

Cliff and Peevy find the rocket pack and switch it on!

Lothar questions Wilmer about the missing rocket pack on behalf of his boss, Neville Sinclair, a Hollywood actor turned Nazi spy.

Air show boss Otis Bigelow declines to reveal to reporters the identity of the new, mysterious "flying man."

Cliff as... The Rocketeer!

Lothar's search for the rocket pack leads him to Cliff and Peevy.

The FBI also winds up at Cliff and Peevy's house.

The Bulldog Cafe—pilot hangout, and now *hideout* for Cliff and Peevy!

The Griffith Observatory where Cliff has agreed to meet Sinclair and swap the rocket pack for his girl Jenny's freedom.

Neville Sinclair prepares to abandon Cliff and Jenny in the burning zeppelin.

Howard Hughes rewards Cliff for his daring by presenting him with a brand-new airplane.

Cliff, Peevy, and Jenny with Peevy's schematic drawing of the now-destroyed rocket pack.

Her ten-year-old daughter, Patsy, tugged on Malcolm's sleeve. She held up a tin airplane. "The wheel came off."

"Lemme see, princess. We'll fix her up," Malcolm said. "Did I ever tell you about the time I was shot by the Red Baron?"

Patsy nodded vigorously, until she caught her mother's "be polite" look. Patsy shifted gears and shook her head no.

"Well, there I was flying patrol . . ." Malcolm began. He fiddled with the toy. Patsy suppressed a yawn. "All of a sudden he comes screaming out of the sun, guns blazing—"

The broken wheel popped out of Malcolm's fingers and splashed in Jenny's soup. Her blouse was ruined!

"Bull's-eye, Ace," Cliff said, fishing the wheel from the soup. Jenny dabbed at her blouse with a napkin.

"I'm sorry, Jenny," Malcolm apologized.

"That's okay," Jenny said. She lowered her voice. "Elegant dining here at the Bulldog. Once in a while it wouldn't hurt to try a new place away from the airfield."

"What'll it be?" Cliff quipped. "The Copa or the Brown Derby? How about the South Seas Club while you're dreaming?"

"Some place an actress could get noticed," Jenny said.

"For the price of one dessert at a place like that I could overhaul an engine!"

"We'll go there after you win the Nationals," Jenny compromised. Cliff nodded reluctantly.

Malcolm swiveled around on his stool. "You are flying in the Nationals? I'm glad to hear it after that landing today," he said. Millie tried to get Malcom to stop talking by offering him some fresh coffee.

"You said there were a few bumps." Jenny wanted Malcolm to say more.

"I'll say!" Malcolm exclaimed. He missed Millie's hint that maybe he should just keep quiet. "Folded like a kite when she hit the pavement. We thought Cliffie's number was up, what with the fire and all."

Millie whacked Malcolm with a spoon. He realized, too late, that he'd said too much. Jenny was furious.

"I was going to tell you," Cliff said lamely, "but

losing his plane is not something a pilot brags about." Jenny just glared at him. Cliff tried another excuse. "I didn't want to spoil our evening."

"When something goes wrong I should be the first to know, not the last," Jenny said icily.

"Honey, everybody else knows because they were there."

"I had an important audition," Jenny said.

"Just like the time I flew the Regionals. You had a big part. You stood behind Myrna Loy with a bowl of grapes."

Jenny threw her napkin down and grabbed her purse.

"Thanks for the soup, Millie," she snapped, and left.

Cliff sat there. Everyone stared at him. He hated himself for making such a mess of things.

"Well, go after her, you dope!" Millie scolded.

Cliff ran outside just in time to see Jenny hop on a bus.

Malcolm walked up behind him. "I'm sorry. I really put my foot in it, didn't I?"

"It's all right," Cliff said. "It's not your fault." He turned and walked back to the Bulldog.

THE FLYING COFFIN

"Cut! Cut! Cut!" the director shouted. Everyone in the movie studio groaned. Once again the producer's "niece" had blown her lines. Jenny should have gotten that part—and Jenny knew it.

"Your audition was so much better," whispered Irma.

"Everybody's audition was better," Jenny told her friend.

Cliff was looking for Jenny. He tripped over cables and banged into light stands as he wandered around behind the scenes. The director called for silence on the set.

Cliff could hear clashing swords and scuffling feet, but he couldn't tell where they were coming from. He peeked through a crack in a wall and saw

Neville Sinclair dueling with another actor. He leaned on the wall to get a better look and discovered it was only a plywood flat.

"Heads up!" someone screamed. The castle wall on the set split and toppled to the floor, exposing Cliff. Suddenly he had a hundred pairs of eyes staring at him.

"Uh . . . sorry. I'm looking for Jenny Blake," he said.

The director forced a big smile. "Is there a Jenny here?"

Jenny timidly raised her hand. She wanted to crawl into a hole. She grabbed Cliff's hand and pulled him off the set.

"Never let it be said that a Neville Sinclair performance failed to bring down the house," Sinclair joked grandly. He turned to the director. "This is supposed to be a closed set. No visitors. I want that girl banned from the lot!"

Cliff tried to apologize to Jenny for the previous night, but he had obviously gotten off to a bad start. To top it off, the assistant director told Jenny she was fired. She fought back tears.

"Lemme explain," Cliff said. "Peevy and I found

something that will get us back on our feet. It's an engine you wear on your back. You can fly like a plane!"

Jenny fumed. "You got me fired to tell me about an engine?"

Before Cliff could say more, he was hustled off the set.

Behind the painted flats, Neville Sinclair had overheard the whole conversation. He hurried to follow, but Cliff was already gone. Thinking fast, Sinclair sought out Jenny.

As he approached her he asked casually, "Have you read the role of the Saxon princess? Perhaps we could discuss the part over dinner at the South Seas Club."

Irma mimed a heart attack. Jenny pretended to be cool, but her heart pounded as she said, "I'd love to."

"If Cliff ain't in the air in five minutes, the deal's off," thundered Bigelow. The air show boss was ready to spit nails.

"He'll be here," Peevy assured him.

Planes roared overhead. The air show was well

under way. Chaplin Airfield was packed with excited spectators, reporters, and newsreel cameras. Mabel waited on the field, but Cliff was nowhere in sight. Peevy nervously checked his watch.

Malcolm overheard Bigelow as he sold programs in the grandstand. He worried about Cliff, until he got an idea!

Meanwhile, behind the bleachers, Spanish Johnny and the rest of Eddie Valentine's gang had some bad news for their boss.

"We searched Hangar Three," Johnny said. "No rocket."

"There was an old plane," Rusty reported. "But the only thing in it was this." He held up Cliff's photo of Jenny.

"So start over," Eddie ordered. "Check every shed and peanut wagon. Keep your eyes peeled for this dame 'Lady Luck.' Maybe she knows the guy who found the rocket."

Spanish Johnny pocketed the photo. "Okay, Mr. Valentine."

Cliff stopped his motorcycle when he saw Mabel lift off the runway. He ran into the grandstand where Peevy and Bigelow were watching the clown act.

"That's not the routine," Bigelow spluttered. "What does Secord think he's doing?"

Just then, Cliff stepped up and asked, "Who's in Mabel?" Bigelow nearly dropped his cigar. Peevy's eyes widened.

"Programs. Get your programs!" a tiny voice squeaked.

All three turned to see Patsy lugging a heavy sack of programs. Malcolm's cap hung over her ears.

"It's Malcolm!" Cliff gasped. "He hasn't flown in twenty-five years!" Bigelow waved his arms to signal the flagman.

"Bring Mabel down!" Bigelow bellowed.

"If he drifts into the race lanes . . ." Peevy began.

Out of control, Mabel swerved into the path of three oncoming racers. Two rolled away; the third climbed hard. Mabel slipped to one side and dove straight for the stands. Spectators ducked as Mabel's wing clipped a flag. Then the plane climbed, engine sputtering and trailing smoke.

"The piston gave out!" Peevy moaned. Cliff

seized his arm and spoke in a low, intense voice. "Peevy, where'd you stash it?" Peevy couldn't peel his eyes from the plane.

"Stash what?" he asked absently.

"You know," Cliff prompted.

"Oh! In the tool chest. Why?" Catching Cliff's meaning, Peevy turned. But Cliff was already racing toward the hangar. Peevy ran after him and found Cliff struggling with the rocket harness.

"What do you think you're doing?" Peevy demanded.

"What's it look like? Give me a hand with this thing."

"We haven't tested it," Peevy objected.

"Cut it out. I'm scared enough as it is." Cliff jogged to the rear doors of the hangar. The heavy pack slapped his spine.

Peevy knew he couldn't stop Cliff. He trotted behind. "Okay, listen. I reworked the throttle. Just give her pressure like a gas pedal. You want to shut her down, punch the button and let go."

"Anything else?" Cliff asked. He grabbed the helmet Peevy had made for use with the rocket pack. It was burnished bronze with a sleek steering fin curved from the crown, tinted amber lenses, and a vertical vent for the mouth.

"Yeah, a little luck." Peevy yanked a wad of gum out of his mouth and slapped it on the rocket's shell.

Cliff buckled the helmet strap. "How do I look?"

"Like a hood ornament," Peevy replied.

Cliff stepped out the hangar door, took a deep breath, and punched the button.

Kablam! He shot into the sky. The blast knocked Peevy down. Barely in control, Cliff soared skyward.

The crowd cheered and shrieked as a flying man suddenly whistled over their heads. Eddie Valentine's jaw dropped. Newsreel cameras swung upward to film the event.

Cliff torpedoed past a racing plane toward Mabel. But he couldn't stop. He smashed headfirst through the cockpit's floor. Malcolm screamed at the sudden arrival of a metal creature between his feet. In panic he grabbed the control stick so hard he ripped it out of the floor, bashing himself between the eyes. He slumped unconscious at the controls.

Meantime, Cliff had been trying to free his helmet from the hole. He succeeded, only to start falling. He grabbed Mabel's landing gear and clung to it desperately.

Inching forward against the buffeting wind, Cliff climbed the lower wing to the cockpit. He couldn't wake Malcolm. Mabel dipped and rolled. Cliff slipped and slid down the wing into empty space.

He fired the rocket and zoomed back to the plane. But the rocket's thrust pushed him toward the plane's propeller. The fin on his helmet touched the blades and sparks flew, while he hooked a toe on the edge of the cockpit.

Cliff shut off his rocket pack. That's when Mabel stalled and started plummeting to the ground in a smoking spiral. Cliff struggled frantically with Malcolm's seat belt. The unconscious man came to in a screaming panic.

"Don't fight me," Cliff cried. "It's me, Cliff!"

But there was no reasoning with the panicked pilot. Malcolm flailed his arms. The control stick smacked Cliff's head. The world whirled upward to meet them. Cliff butted Malcolm with his helmet, and threw his arms around the now-unconscious pilot.

“Come on, you tub of guts,” Cliff muttered. He hit the rocket pack’s red button again. He ripped Malcolm out of Mabel, seat and all. They punched through the top wing in a shower of shattered wood.

Kaboom! The airfield rocked. Bigelow’s brand-new fuel truck exploded as Mabel met her doom. Bigelow almost swallowed his cigar. Cliff rose from the rising ball of flame, dipped over the cheering spectators, and dropped Malcolm gently on the runway. Then he blasted off.

Dazed, Malcolm discovered himself safely on the ground, still strapped in the seat. Flashbulbs popped. Malcolm grinned and raised the control stick above his head.

“What I wouldn’t pay for that act!” Bigelow exclaimed.

“Five hundred bucks a show?” Peevy said.

“Easy!” Bigelow stared dumbfounded after the flying man.

“We’ll take it,” Peevy said. Bigelow shot him a stunned look. He realized Peevy had just negotiated a deal.

“You mean to tell me that’s—” Bigelow began.

"You don't know who he is. That's part of the deal," Peevy said. He ran to his truck and took off after Cliff.

Eddie and his boys piled into their cars, honking at the crowd in their way. They had plans for the flying man, too.

Cliff burst through a puffy white cloud and came upon a passenger plane. Astonished faces pressed to the windows. Cliff saluted a pretty stewardess—and spiraled wildly out of control! He swooped through a yard and snared himself in a clean sheet flapping on a clothesline.

Looking like a ghost, Cliff zipped through an orchard before peeling off the sheet. He smashed a fence and plowed across a cornfield. Bursting free of the stalks, he almost collided with Peevy's speeding truck. Peevy swerved one way and Cliff skipped like a stone across the surface of a pond.

Peevy jumped from the truck and raced to the steaming water. A very wet Cliff sat in a nest of crushed reeds.

"You had to show off!" Peevy scolded. "Lucky

you didn't break your neck." He pulled off the helmet. Cliff grinned from ear to ear. "How was it, kid?" Peevy said.

Cliff sighed. "Closest I'll ever get to heaven."

Peevy had to smile, too. "Gotta work on those landings."

They started back to the truck. They heard approaching engines. Peevy said, "Must be the newsboys."

Cliff looked alarmed. "They can't find out who we are."

Peevy and Cliff drove off. But it wasn't reporters. It was Eddie Valentine's gang, and as Peevy's truck rattled away they wrote down the license number.

6

WHO IS THE ROCKETEER?

In the clutter of Bigelow's shabby office, reporters shoved and shouted. "Where'd you find the flying man?"

"What's his name?" a news hawk demanded.

Bigelow shook his head. "Sorry, fellas, it's part of the mystery. Let's just call him . . . Rocket Boy."

"That's lousy," the first reporter complained.

"How about 'The Human Rocket'?" someone suggested.

"That stinks!" another reporter said.

Bigelow's mind raced. He was too excited to think. "Uh . . . how's about Rocketeer?" he stammered.

"Rocketeer, that's swell!"

News of the mysterious "Rocketeer" was plastered over every newspaper's front page the next day.

WHO IS THE ROCKETEER? one headline screamed. Neville Sinclair's eyes bulged. Dazed, he lowered his newspaper. This was bad news indeed. The secret was out!

ROCKETEER SAVES PILOT said the paper on Howard Hughes's desk. Hughes removed a dirty blanket covering a pile of charred metal. He shoved the wreckage across the floor toward the feet of FBI agents Wooly and Fitch. "Congratulations, gentlemen. Due to the diligence of the FBI, this vacuum cleaner did not fall into the wrong hands," he said angrily.

Wooly and Fitch hurried off to the airfield, where they planned to confront Bigelow about his new star performer.

"Mr. Bigelow, FBI," Wooly said, knocking on Bigelow's office door. "We'd like to have a word with you." The door creaked open. Wooly and Fitch entered cautiously. The place had been ransacked! In the light of the desk lamp, they saw emptied drawers and papers scattered everywhere.

On the floor lay Bigelow's lifeless form, a pencil still in his hand. A notepad was on his desk. By tilting the pad under the light, the agents made out the impression of the last thing Bigelow had written: 1635 Palm Terrace.

Lothar's huge shape shadowed the lawn at 1635 Palm Terrace as he crept to the porch.

In the kitchen, Peevy was finishing a detailed schematic drawing of the rocket pack. The sleek helmet rested nearby, the dents from Cliff's rescue of Malcolm all smoothed out. Peevy inserted a funnel in the rocket's fuel port and topped the tank with alcohol. Suddenly he heard a creaking on the back stairs.

Cliff's motorcycle pulled up in front of the house. He couldn't wait to show Peevy the newspapers. Sounds of a struggle made him drop everything and run up the steps.

"Peevy!" he shouted, pounding on the locked door. Through the door's window Cliff could see

Lothar. He was about to break the door when it swung open and he fell in. Lothar lifted him from the floor.

"Where's the rocket?" Lothar growled. Cliff's eyes quickly searched the room and found the pack on a table. Clever Peevy had disguised it with a shade to look like a fancy lamp.

"Sure you got the right house?" Cliff asked.

A pack of police cars pulled up on the lawn.

"Secord! Peabody! Open up! FBI!" Fitch ordered.

Lothar dropped Cliff and drew two guns. He began firing at the FBI. Cliff and Peevy hit the deck. Tommy guns and pistols answered Lothar's volley. Bullets splintered the house. On his way to the back door, Lothar grabbed Peevy's rocket pack plans from the kitchen table. He demolished the door and ran off. Cliff and Peevy scrambled out too, clutching the rocket pack.

Jenny pinched herself to see if she was dreaming. She would never forget stepping onto the red carpet, or the dazzle of camera flashbulbs, or the press of autograph hounds as she walked with Neville Sinclair into the South Seas Club.

The place was even more beautiful than she had imagined. Fishnet hung from the ceiling. Palm trees swayed beneath a stained-glass skylight. A band played near a giant clamshell and a woman done up like a mermaid swam in a tank. Marble dolphins curved outward from bunches of ferns. A galaxy of movie stars in crisp tuxedos and glamorous gowns sparkled at linen-and-crystal-covered tables.

Once they were seated, a man whispered to Sinclair. The actor excused himself and went upstairs to see the club's owner, Eddie Valentine.

"My boys are tearing up the town looking for this Cliff Secord and you waltz in here with this dame," said Eddie. "What gives?"

"That 'dame' is Secord's girl," Sinclair explained.

Eddie scowled. "Why're you always keeping me in the dark? My boys finally tracked down Secord and your ape's already been there. The place was crawling with Feds. Now you've got a hook in his girlfriend and I'm the last to know."

"I'm running out of time. I'll do what I have to

do to get my hands on that device—and so will you!" Sinclair said.

"You don't know who you're talking to," Eddie snarled.

"A small-time hoodlum with big-time plans," Sinclair said. "I could demolish your shabby little empire with a phone call."

"I could make a call of my own," Eddie threatened.

Sinclair sneered. "Who would they believe? A known criminal or the number-three box-office star in America?"

"Call the FBI and give the rocket back," Peevy said. He and Cliff were huddled in the attic of the Bulldog Café.

"The FBI just tore our house in half," Cliff argued. "They think we were shooting at them. They'll lock us up!"

There was a knock on the trapdoor in the floor. A worried Malcolm poked his head up and reported, "Somebody tore up Bigelow's office looking for something. They killed him!"

Shaken by the news, Cliff decided that things had gotten way out of hand. He climbed down from the attic and headed for the phone to call the FBI. Just then Spanish Johnny and a pack of thugs in expensive suits walked into the café. They wanted Cliff, but no one in the café would squeal. Cliff stood by the phone, watching, while Spanish Johnny and the boys began to play rough with the customers.

Then Spanish Johnny spotted Jenny's name scrawled on the wall by the pay phone. He pulled Jenny's photo from his pocket. "Look at this, boys! Lady Luck left her phone number." He dialed the number and pretended to be a florist with a delivery for Jenny. Irma told him Jenny was at the South Seas Club with Neville Sinclair.

"Rusty! This'll slay ya. The dame is with Sinclair at the South Seas Club." Johnny laughed. "You guys stay here and watch what walks in. We'll call from the club." He and Rusty left.

While Cliff and his buddies looked on, the gangsters stole doughnuts and idly played with their guns. One of them began looking at the pictures of pilots decorating the café walls. Everyone tensed as he got closer and closer to a photo of Cliff and Jenny.

"That's 'Lady Luck,' " the thug said, and turned to Cliff. "That makes you—" Before he could finish, Cliff and his friends swung into action. Frying pans and fists flew fast and furious. Shots ricocheted wildly from the thugs' guns, but soon the gangsters were beaten. Cliff and Peevy left Skeets to guard them, and raced back up to the attic. Cliff strapped on the rocket pack.

"Not again! We've gotta give it back!" Peevy protested.

"I'm sorry, but Jenny's in trouble . . . and I love her!" Cliff said. He was about to blast off when Peevy spotted fuel leaking from the dented rocket.

"Wait! You'll blow us all up! It must've caught a bullet during all the commotion."

"Can you patch it?" Cliff asked.

His mind racing, Peevy saw the wad of gum stuck on the rocket.

"How about a little luck?" he asked, jamming it over the bullet hole. "Promise me when Jenny's safe you'll give it back."

Cliff put on the helmet. "Stand clear!"

Peevy was bowled over by the blastoff. Cliff streaked into the sky like a shooting star. Peevy picked himself up from a pile of cans and looked into the shiny muzzle of a massive gun. He raised his hands and froze in fear.

7

DOLPHINS AND DANGER

"It's all so elegant," Jenny sighed. Just last night she was in a greasy diner with soup on her blouse. Now she sat with famous movie star Neville Sinclair at a table in the South Seas Club. She confessed to Neville that she had never been to the swanky restaurant before. Neville admitted to living on baloney sandwiches while beginning his career as an extra.

"You must let me have this dance," Sinclair said.

Jenny looked around, confused. "There's no music."

"Really?" Sinclair asked. "I hear music."

He led Jenny to the quiet, empty dance floor. He took her in his arms and they danced. Other patrons watched with hushed wonder.

The bandleader peeked from behind the curtain to see why the club was suddenly silent. "Break time's over!" he told his band. Musicians hurriedly took their places and began to play. For Jenny, it was a dream come true!

In a flash of light, a shadow dropped into an alley behind the club. Smoke drifted in the air. Cliff removed his pack and helmet and stuffed them in a duffel bag. He couldn't enter the club without evening dress, so he slipped in through a service door in back, and ducked into the laundry room. He hastily hid his bag in a laundry sack. Then he took a busboy's uniform from a rack, pulled it over his clothes, passed through the kitchen, and entered the club. When he saw Sinclair and Jenny twirling in a spotlight, his jaw tightened. So that's how it was!

When the dance was over, Sinclair and Jenny returned to their table. A cloud passed over Jenny's beautiful face. She missed Cliff. She remembered how often they had talked about coming here.

"I know that look, Jenny. Is it your boyfriend?" Sinclair asked. "Tell me about my competition."

"Well, he's a little rough around the edges," Jenny began. "But sometimes he's the sweetest guy in the world."

Sinclair steered Jenny with crafty questions until she told him about Cliff's crash the day before. She was interrupted by a soup bowl being thumped down on the table. Sinclair protested that they hadn't ordered yet. The waiter told him a fan had sent the soup.

He set a bowl before Jenny. Hers held a note: "Meet me by the big fish now!" Jenny looked up. The waiter was Cliff! He motioned toward a large statue of a dolphin. He ladled hot soup on top of the note.

Jenny was upset. How dare Cliff try to ruin her special date! She deliberately ignored Cliff's note and furtive gestures.

"Where is your boyfriend now?" Sinclair asked.

"Hatching some harebrained scheme—" Jenny snipped. He's working on an engine a man can strap—" She broke off.

Desperate, Cliff had poured cold champagne in her lap. Jenny had to get up, and Cliff had protected his secret.

At the dolphin statue, Cliff pulled Jenny into a thicket of potted palms. Jenny thought Cliff was just jealous until he told her Bigelow had been murdered by men seeking the rocket.

"They have your picture from the GeeBee," Cliff warned. "Get ready for a shock. I'm the Rocketeer."

"The Rocka-who?" Jenny was puzzled.

Disappointed, Cliff asked, "Haven't you seen the papers?"

"I've been locked away on a soundstage all day."

"It doesn't matter. Get in a cab. Go to your mother's," Cliff said. "Stay there until you hear from me."

Jenny searched his eyes. "Why should I believe this?"

"Because if anything happened to you I'd go crazy!" Cliff said, tender pleading in his eyes. They kissed. Then Cliff saw Spanish Johnny and Rusty enter the club.

"That's them," Cliff hissed. "The ones with the photo."

With a brave smile, Jenny headed for the front door. As she went out one side, Lothar lurched in the other. Startled patrons gave the grotesque giant a wide berth. Jenny waved for a taxi.

Cliff was about to sneak back out of the club when he saw Spanish Johnny and Rusty talking to Sinclair. The gangsters seemed to be taking orders from the movie star. Was Sinclair after the rocket? Before Cliff could think, he found himself face to face with Lothar. Cliff dashed across the dance floor. Lothar pushed people aside in pursuit.

The giant rammed through the restaurant like an express train, leaving a trail of tossed trays and trampled toes. Cliff barely made it to the laundry room. Breathless, he bolted the door. He turned to grab his hidden duffel bag—but twenty fresh laundry sacks had been added to the pile. Where was the rocket pack? Cliff searched frantically, while Lothar thumped at the door.

Lothar succeeded in tearing the door from its hinges and charged into the room like an angry bull. But it was empty! All he saw were sacks of soiled tablecloths. Then he spotted a pair of boots in the laundry chute. He grabbed for them. *Ka-blam!* He was blown off his feet by the rocket's blast.

Cliff shot up the chute and into the club through the ladies' lounge. He bounced off walls and skimmed the ceiling, scattering dishes and torching tables. Panicked people stampeded to the exits. Sinclair watched in shock, then shouted to Spanish Johnny, "Close those doors! He's trapped! Shoot him down!"

Gunshots peppered the club. Smoke filled the room. All the exits were sealed. Cliff swooped in circles. Eddie Valentine tried to stop the destruction of his club, but Sinclair was determined to get that rocket!

A stray bullet shattered the mermaid tank. Water gushed out, sweeping Eddie downstairs along with a flopping mermaid. Singed and seething, Lothar emerged from the service door.

Cliff slid down the bar, shattering glasses in his wake. He slammed into an ice sculpture of a huge snail. Seizing its eyestalks, he jumped on and sledded for the exit.

"He's got a battering ram!" one of Eddie's men shouted.

Sinclair grabbed his gun. Bullets sprayed the ice and the snail's eyestalks snapped off. Without his steering handles, Cliff couldn't stay aboard. He raced away, leaving the melting sculpture to crash through the front door.

Frightened South Seas Club patrons began to pour through the opening. The rush of people pushed Jenny away from her long-awaited taxi. *Only Cliff could make this much trouble,* Jenny thought. *He needs me!* She fought her way through the crowd back into the club and hid behind a column, searching for Cliff through the smoke.

Cliff aimed for the open doors, just as Sinclair dropped the fishnet from the ceiling. Snared, Cliff crashed to the floor. He cut his engine.

"Get the rocket!" Sinclair demanded. Lothar advanced, squeezing Cliff in a deadly embrace. But the palms parted and a plaster seahorse smashed down on Lothar's skull. Jenny grinned and sank back into the bushes. The giant groaned and dropped.

Eddie's men closed in on Cliff, but he blasted off through the skylight. Colored glass rained down. Cliff spiraled up past whizzing bullets. One grazed his helmet. Jenny ran for the door, but was snatched by Sinclair.

"Don't go," said Sinclair smoothly. "Our evening has just begun."

The neighborhood was dark and quiet. The Bulldog Café loomed large and pale in the moonlight. Cliff crept in through the back door. He climbed a few steps of the storeroom ladder and lifted the attic trapdoor to look into the Bulldog's head. "Peevy? Millie?" Cliff called.

"Hey, Cliff!" Patsy yelled from below.

Startled, Cliff dropped the trapdoor on his head and fell off the ladder. "You scared me!" he said. "Where's Peevy?"

"Some men took him away."

Cliff looked at Patsy in shock. He jumped when the phone rang. He snatched up the receiver. "Peevy?"

But it was Eddie Valentine. "If you wanna see Jenny again, meet me at the Griffith Observatory at four A.M., by the statues. Bring the rocket. Come alone or your girl's dead."

Cliff was confused. He thought Jenny was at her mother's, but Eddie put her on the phone to prove she was his captive.

Patsy was frightened. "What are they doing to Jenny?"

"Quiet! I have to think," Cliff snapped, jotting notes on a pad. Patsy tried not to cry. Cliff knelt down remorsefully to comfort her. "I didn't mean to yell at you. Can you keep a big secret?" Patsy nodded. "You know the flying man who saved Malcolm today? He's going to help me get Jenny back."

Patsy looked excitedly at Cliff and dried her tears. "The Rocketeer can do anything!" she cried.

Cliff wasn't so sure, but when he saw the look in her eyes, he answered, "Yeah. Maybe he can." Patsy hugged him tight.

Suddenly both doors of the café burst open. Four armed men rushed in. Patsy and Cliff were surrounded! Then Fitch stepped into the light and smiled. "Remember me?"

Woozy, Jenny woke in the master bedroom of Neville Sinclair's mansion. The door was locked. Through a glass panel she could see Sinclair slip from a secret room behind a revolving bookcase.

He came into the room. Jenny said accusingly, "You kidnapped me!"

"The gangsters forced me to do it," Sinclair lied. "But they can be reasoned with if they get what they want."

Jenny pretended to believe him. She listened to Sinclair try to flatter her, but she recognized most of his lines from his old movies. As Sinclair continued to talk, Jenny eyed a pitcher on the night table next to the bed. In an instant, she lunged for the pitcher and broke it over Sinclair's head. Then she ran for her life.

Lothar blocked the front door. Searching for another exit, Jenny ducked into the secret room. She tried to raise help on the radio but was answered in German! A Nazi codebook lay on the table, beside Peevy's plans for the rocket pack. Jenny took the plans and hid them in her gown. She came to a terrible realization. Stunned, she said out loud, "Oh, no! Neville Sinclair is a—"

"A spy? A saboteur? A Nazi?" Neville prompted from the doorway. "All of the above!"

"So all I did was bypass the pressure valve," Peevy told Howard Hughes. "That solved your throttle problem."

"Adding a rudder to the helmet was ingenious," Hughes said with admiration.

"Nah, just basic aviation," Peevy said modestly.

Cliff was led into the room by Fitch. "No sign of the rocket. He's not talking," the G-man said.

Hughes rose. "I designed the Cirrus X-3, the rocket pack. It was stolen from my factory."

"I didn't steal it, Mr. Hughes," Cliff said. Every pilot recognized the famous aircraft designer.

"I told him the whole deal," Peevy said. "Mr. Hughes believes us. Give him the rocket."

"I can't do that," Cliff said anxiously.

In an effort to persuade Cliff, Hughes showed a film of the Nazi plan to use the rocket pack to conquer the world.

"I can slap you with grand theft, espionage, treason!" Fitch shouted. "And that's just my short list."

"They've got my girl," Cliff explained at last. "If anything happens to her, I don't care about the rest of the world. I'll return the pack tomorrow. I can deal with the Valentine gang."

"Valentine is only hired muscle," Hughes said. "They work for a Nazi agent our G-men have been unable to identify."

"It's Neville Sinclair," Cliff said.

"Nice try, kid," Wooly scoffed. "I don't like his movies, either. We'll take him downtown and lock him up."

Cliff leaped up and grabbed a giant model airplane on an overhead track. He rode it down the track and smashed through the windows to freedom. The note from his talk with Eddie Valentine dropped to the carpet: Griffith Obs. 4 A.M.

8

FIRE IN THE SKIES

It was close to four in the morning and the sky was clear. Moonlight splashed over the white walls and copper domes of the Griffith Observatory. Behind the building, cliffs dropped off sheer and straight above the sleeping city.

In the center of the dark lawn stood statues of famous astronomers. At their marble feet, Valentine's gang waited impatiently for Neville Sinclair.

When the movie star arrived, Lothar dragged Jenny from the auto. Sinclair handed her his tuxedo jacket. "Put this on."

"I'd rather freeze," Jenny said, shivering.

"Suit yourself," Sinclair said. He looked at Eddie Valentine. "Cheer up! You're about to make a fortune."

A distant whine drew all eyes skyward. A shooting star streaked through the night, growing larger and brighter. The gangsters pointed their tommy guns.

Cliff landed on the grass under the gangsters' wary gaze. He lifted his helmet and faced the thicket of gun barrels.

"Jenny, are you all right?" he asked. She nodded bravely.

"Take off the rocket," Sinclair ordered. "Carefully."

"When you let Jenny go," Cliff responded. He had a plan.

Eddie sighed. "Hand it over so we can all go home."

Cliff looked at Eddie. "What's it like working for a Nazi?"

Eddie looked confused. Sinclair was barely able to conceal his shock.

Cliff nodded. "I heard it straight from the Feds."

"He's been flying where the air's too thin," Sinclair said in an attempt to bluff. He sneaked a peek at his watch.

"Ask him about the secret room and the Germans

on the radio," Jenny urged. Eddie studied her earnest face. He never had trusted Sinclair.

"I may not be honest, but I'm one hundred percent American," Eddie declared. His gang's guns trained their muzzles on Sinclair and Lothar. "Let the lady go."

Sinclair was defiant. "I'm still taking the rocket."

Eddie laughed. "You and what army?"

Sinclair snapped a sentence in German. Twenty commandos in Nazi uniforms burst from the bushes, surrounding the observatory.

Sinclair flashed a serpent grin. "Your move, Eddie."

A huge silver zeppelin sank from the clouds. On its side was the name: LUXEMBOURG. So much for its "goodwill tour" of the U.S., Cliff thought, remembering the newsreel he and Jenny had seen.

Sinclair gave more orders in German and a commando ran to remove the pack from Cliff's back. Suddenly spotlights from screeching police cars lit the scene as FBI agents spilled from sedans.

Led by Fitch and Wooly, the lawmen leaped into position.

Fitch yelled, "This is the FBI. Throw down your guns!"

Cliff seized that moment to ignite the rocket pack. The fiery engine dragged him and the helpless Nazi commando across the lawn and over a ledge.

A furious gun battle erupted. On one side were the Nazi commandos and on the other the lawmen and the gangsters.

Lothar blasted away, protecting Sinclair and his hostage, Jenny. The three climbed to the observatory roof.

On the roof, Lothar mounted a rope ladder lowered from the zeppelin. Sinclair pushed Jenny toward Lothar, who pulled her kicking and screaming into the airship.

Inside the gondola part of the airship, Sinclair assured a Nazi agent that as long as they had Jenny, Cliff would deliver the rocket pack. "Now get this ship above the clouds!" he barked.

Down below, with the help of Valentine's gang, lawmen rounded up the defeated Nazis. But Fitch and Wooly watched with dismay as the zeppelin rose high into the predawn sky.

Recovered from his rocky ride, Cliff grabbed a fallen pistol and climbed back up the hillside. He scooped up his helmet and ran to the top of the observatory. He streaked like a flaming arrow after the fleeing zeppelin.

The zeppelin grew larger as The Rocketeer rushed to meet it. He eased off the throttle. But in his eagerness to reach Jenny, Cliff misjudged his speed and smacked into the zeppelin's tail. Fabric ripped under the impact, and the rushing wind made the hole still larger as the rudder swung and flapped in the breeze.

Cliff fell on the airship's arched body, then pulled himself to his feet. He fought the wind all the way to a hatch.

In the gondola below, Sinclair watched the pilot and crewmen struggle to control the rocking airship.

The captain cried, "Something's wrong with the rudder!"

A spark of hope ignited in Jenny's heart.

Atop the zeppelin, as Cliff reached the maintenance hatch, it popped open revealing Lothar. Instantly, Lothar knocked Cliff's pistol away, then hooked a safety tether to his own belt. Cliff and Lothar began to battle on the zeppelin's slippery surface. Cliff lost his balance and fell, but zipped up again on blazing jets and knocked Lothar over the side.

Lothar swung like a wrecking ball through the gondola's window. The pilot was bumped through the door into the void.

Sinclair shouted, "Do I have to fly the ship myself?!"

The captain panicked. "We're losing altitude. We must drop some weight from the gondola."

Without a second's thought, Sinclair shot the Nazi agent and pushed him out the door.

Cliff dropped down the roof hatch and knocked out the last crewman.

Wild-eyed, Sinclair pointed a gun at Jenny's head. "I've had a bellyful of your cheap heroics. Hand over the rocket," he ordered Cliff.

"Don't give it to him," Jenny urged.

"I have to," Cliff said. He unbuckled the pack. As he stooped to set the rocket on the floor, he secretly plucked the wad of gum from the fuel tank. Then he pushed the pack across the floor to Sinclair.

Sinclair shoved Jenny into the captain's arms and handed the captain his pistol. "If she moves, shoot her."

Jenny fumed. "If one more man puts a gun to my head . . ."

The captain pointed the pistol. Jenny drove a spiked heel into his foot. She pushed the Nazi against the control panel and kicked his gun out the door.

Cliff and Sinclair struggled with each other.

"Where's your stuntman now?" Cliff taunted.

Sinclair replied, fists flying, "I do my own stunts!"

The battling men bounced against an emergency box. Jenny picked up a large-barreled pistol from the spilled contents. She aimed her trembling hands at Sinclair.

"Stop! I'll shoot!" Jenny threatened. Shaking sweat and blood from his eyes, Cliff saw the flare gun in Jenny's hand.

"Jenny! No!" Cliff cried. One blast from the flare gun would ignite the whole gas-filled ship.

Sinclair lunged at the girl. Jenny pulled the trigger. The flaming flare bounced a blazing path through the gondola. Cliff frantically grabbed a fire extinguisher. Smoke filled the cabin.

"Sinclair! Help us put out the fire," he shouted.

The licking flames spread faster and faster. Sinclair laughed in the gondola door. He was wearing the rocket pack.

"Good-bye! I'm going to miss Hollywood," the actor called.

"Don't be so sure," Cliff said.

The spy leaped into space and ignited the rocket. The Hollywood Hills spread below him, and he could see the famous HOLLYWOODLAND sign. But fuel began to spray from the leak in the rocket's fuel tank. The pack burst into flame, sending Sinclair like a blazing comet straight into the giant sign. There was a tremendous explosion, and the last four letters vanished, leaving the sign to read HOLLYWOOD.

Cliff helped Jenny clamber through the maintenance hatch. They stood atop the zeppelin. Cliff held Jenny, protecting her from the wind.

"This thing's full of hydrogen," Cliff said. "When the fire hits the envelope . . ."

"I love you, Cliff!" Jenny said. They shared a last kiss.

But with a whirr of an engine, an odd aircraft suddenly appeared. It looked like a plane with a helicopter rotor. Inside the strange machine were Howard Hughes and Peevy. Howard Hughes struggled to hold his autogyro steady while Peevy lowered a ladder to Cliff and Jenny.

But Lothar had just managed to haul himself up his tether. He blocked Cliff and Jenny's path to the ladder.

Suddenly Lothar paled as a sizzling fireball from the burning zeppelin rolled toward them. Cliff, Jenny, and Lothar all ran for the ladder. Tied by his tether, Lothar fumbled with the release clip. A tidal wave of flame surged over him.

Peevy yelled at the top of his lungs, "Jump for it!" Jenny wrapped her arms around Cliff's neck. He leaped for the swinging ladder. The autogyro banked away just as the zeppelin exploded.

9

ROCKETEER TO THE RESCUE!

AIRSHIP DISASTER OVER HOLLYWOOD HILLS

Peevy Peabody was surprised to read the story beneath the headline. According to the paper, the explosion was caused by a freak bolt of lightning which destroyed the zeppelin LUXEMBOURG! Film fans were saddened by news that actor Neville Sinclair also perished when flaming debris fell on his car.

"What a shame!" Peevy dunked a doughnut. "Nice car." He was sharing a booth in the Bulldog Café with Cliff and Jenny. Lost in thought, Cliff stared out the window.

Jenny said, "You look sad for a guy who saved the world."

"I've got the cracked ribs to prove it," Cliff said ruefully. "And not much else."

Jenny scooted closer and rested her chin on his shoulder. "You've got me." He smiled slowly as he gazed into her eyes.

Suddenly a familiar droning filled the sky. Dishes rattled on the counter. Cliff jumped to his feet and rushed outside, but the sound was already fading. He stood in the gravel driveway searching the sky. Jenny was quick to follow. "What is it?"

"Sounded like a racer," Cliff said wistfully. "I missed her, though. Guess she's landing in the field." He strained to hear the distant engine. Jenny took his hand to lead him back inside. But a shiny blue limousine rounded the corner and stopped before the Bulldog. Two men leaped out and cleared the street of autos and pedestrians.

The roar of a plane engine grew louder. A brand-new GeeBee racer taxied around the street corner. Its black-and-white finish gleamed as it eased to a stop and Howard Hughes climbed from the cockpit. Jenny and Cliff approached the plane. Peevy and the rest of the regulars came out of the Bulldog.

"She's a beauty, Mr. Hughes," Cliff said.

"Thanks. Built her myself," Hughes replied. "By

next month she'll be ready for the Nationals." He smiled at Jenny. "Miss Blake, would you excuse me for a moment?"

"Of course," Jenny said. Hughes pulled Cliff a few steps to the side. The millionaire leaned in close. "What was it like, strapping that thing to your back and flying like a hawk?"

Cliff glanced at Jenny. "It was the second closest thing to heaven." Hughes laughed and shook Cliff's hand.

"See ya 'round, Rocketeer!" the tycoon cried. He started back to his limousine, then turned and tossed a pack of gum to Cliff. "Don't fly her without this," Hughes warned.

Cliff caught the gum and looked confused. Hughes's assistant pulled a strip of tape from the rim of the GeeBee's cockpit. Beneath the sticky strip was hand-lettering: PILOT: CLIFF SECORD.

A wide grin formed on Cliff's face. He was too happy to speak. He turned to thank Hughes, but the limo was already pulling away. All he saw was Hughes's hand waving.

Jenny, Peevy, and the gang joined to admire the gleaming new racer.

"I . . . didn't get a chance to thank him," Cliff stammered.

"He saw it in your face, kid," Peevy assured him.

"I have something for you, too," Jenny said. "Actually, it's Peevy's." She took a piece of paper from her purse and gave it to the mechanic. He unfolded it and looked surprised.

"Oh no!" Peevy cried. It was his drawings of the rocket pack. He shook his head in bewilderment. Cliff laughed. He swept Jenny up in a joyful embrace.